Winning the REAL Prize!

AT THE
EASTER EGG HUNT

David Forden — A story of a young boy learning the value of kindness and sharing.

Themes:
1. Kindness and sharing
2. Overcoming disappointment
3. Joy in doing acts of generosity
4. Importance of parental affirmation
5. Practice of empathy

Written and Illustrated by: David H. Forden

Published by: Marmoset Press

Contact us: MarmosetPress@gmail.com

Printed in the United States of America

ISBN: 978-1-7331163-0-5

Winning the REAL Prize!

AT THE
EASTER EGG HUNT

WRITTEN & ILLUSTRATED by DAVID FORDEN

It was the biggest Easter basket Scotty had ever

seen. A giant basket bursting with candies and fun

prizes had been donated for the Easter egg hunt on

Saturday morning.

The basket and the prizes would go to the child

who collected the most eggs.

Scotty was so excited, all he could think

about was winning the giant Easter basket.

He had his own Easter basket to collect all

the eggs he hoped to find. He wanted to

find as many eggs as he could.

This is going to be fun!

The night before the Easter egg hunt it was hard for Scotty to go to sleep.

He dreamed of finding the Easter eggs and winning the giant basket, the biggest prize he had ever seen.

At breakfast, all Scotty could think about was where he was going to discover the most Easter eggs. He thought the eggs could be anywhere.

They could be next to a rock. They could be under a bush. They could be *in* the bush. They could be in a tree. They could be next to a hole in the ground where a bunny lives.

They could be anywhere!

When Scotty and his parents arrived at the church, there were a lot of children at the Easter egg hunt.

All the kids had their own Easter baskets. Everyone had his or her eye on winning the giant basket.

The boys and girls lined up to start the

Easter egg hunt. The starting bell rang —

the children ran in every direction.

But Scotty had a plan. He ran to a spot at the

far end of the yard and did not stop to pick up

any eggs along the way.

Because he was the first to arrive at the spot,

wherever he looked he found Easter eggs!

Scotty was a genuine Easter egg magnet.

He found Easter eggs surrounding him

everywhere, waiting to be found.

Before long Scotty's basket was

overflowing with eggs.

He was going to win the basket full

of prizes!

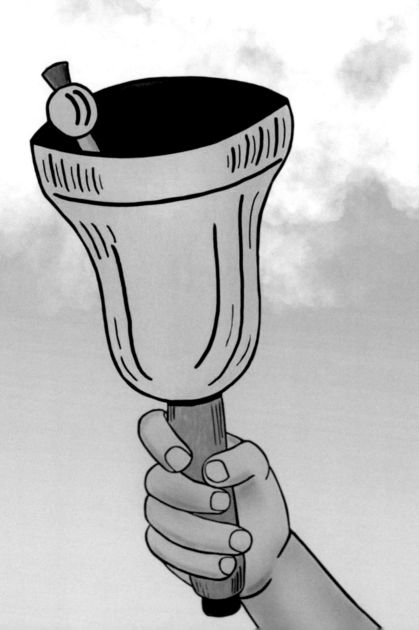

The ending bell rang, signaling the kids

to gather for the egg count. It was time

to see who won the big prize.

Scotty spotted an unhappy little girl carefully holding an empty basket. As he looked at her, he felt a little sad. He wondered if she would like some of his eggs.

At that moment Scotty decided what he was going to do.

Scotty took two eggs from his basket and gave them to her. Her frown changed into a big smile, her eyes joyful and bright.

Scotty smiled as well. He was surprised that sharing his eggs could make them both happy.

There were a few other boys and girls who returned with empty baskets. Scotty knew what he was going to do.

He smiled and shared his treasured eggs from his own basket.

His basket began to feel lighter and so did

his heart. He never knew sharing would

feel this good.

The official egg counting began. Scotty still had a very full basket of eggs.

And at the final egg count . . .

Scotty was just *one* egg short of winning the big prize. He could hardly believe it. He was only one egg away from winning the largest basket he'd ever seen.

Scotty slumped his shoulders, feeling disappointed at the loss.

Scotty walked over to his dad and his dad hugged him. "You did a great job collecting *and* sharing your eggs."

Scotty nodded his head but didn't feel like he had done anything great.

His dad gently asked, "Why did you give

away your Easter eggs to the other children?"

Scotty glanced up. "But Dad, I had so many Easter eggs in my basket and they didn't have any."

His dad smiled with a twinkle in his eye. "So it was important to share with those who had nothing?"

"Yes. It was!" Scotty began feeling pleased and happy again.

"Even if you didn't win the Giant Prize Easter Basket?"

"I didn't like that part." Scotty shrugged. "But yes, it *was* important *to me*. The other kids were so sad. I thought it was the right thing to do."

His dad patted his shoulder. "I think so, too."

Scotty was quiet for a moment, the joy

growing in his chest again. "Easter isn't

just about collecting eggs and winning

a prize, is it?"

The smile on his father's face grew wide.

"You are right, Scotty. It is about so much more than that."

He nodded his head, adding, "I think the real prize is what we feel in our hearts when we show love and kindness to others."

"Do you know what I think? I think it is about caring enough for other kids to see they get some Easter eggs too, even if I didn't win the giant basket."

Dad hugged Scotty again, beaming with pride. "I am more proud of you for sharing your eggs with the other children than if you won a truckload of giant baskets."

On his way back home, Scotty felt very happy inside.

In Scotty's heart, he felt like he had won the **real prize** that day.

The End

About the Author:

David Forden has had the good fortune to celebrate his life as a husband, son, father, brother, minister, U. S. Army Reserves Chaplain and Licensed Marriage and Family Therapist. He lives in California with his lovely bride Annie, without whom this book would not be possible.

Acknowledgements:

While on one of my assignments in Garmisch, Germany, a lay leader of the Chapel told a story about his son sharing his Easter eggs with other children.

Thank you, John and Scott, for inspiring this book.

Made in the USA
San Bernardino, CA
22 June 2019